The Last Summer

Karen Swan is a *Sunday Times* top three bestselling author and her novels sell all over the world. She writes two books each year – one for the summer period and one for the Christmas season.

Her books are known for their vivid locations and Karen sees travel as vital research for each story. She loves to set deep, complicated love stories within twisting plots.

Her historical series, called The Wild Isle, is based upon the dramatic evacuation of the Scottish island St Kilda in the summer of 1930.

**Thanks to your help,
we're getting the nation reading!**

One in six adults in the UK struggles with reading. Buying this Quick Read could change someone's life. For every Quick Read sold, a copy will be donated to someone who finds reading difficult. From mental health to social mobility, reading has a proven positive impact on life's big challenges. Find out more: readingagency.org.uk @readingagency #QuickReads

Karen Swan

The Last Summer

PAN BOOKS

For Laura Tinkl, who is part of our story now

13 May 1930

Before

Chapter One

Effie Gillies watched as the ship slipped into the bay.

Her eyes were fixed on the black dots as the visitors moved from one vessel to the other. She and the other islanders all knew the drill. Once they had dried off, they would want a show. And she was going to give it to them.

Effie looped the rope around the peg. She leant back, checking its firmness and tension. She wrapped it around her waist. Then she looked down the drop.

'First to the boat then?' Angus thought he was the fastest climber on the island.

'Yes,' she told him. 'But I'll wait for you, don't worry.'

Angus's eyes narrowed at her insult, but she was already off. Down she went.

She glanced up. Angus was only a few feet above her. She looked carefully back over her shoulder. The rowboat was tied to a rock just a short distance away.

She twisted and leapt blind. Death or glory then!

For one moment, she felt almost as if she could fly. Then the force of gravity took over. She landed – half in the rowboat, half in the water. She laughed as her Uncle Hamish dragged her aboard in one swift movement.

'Do females climb here, too?' the older visitor asked their skipper.

'Only this one.' Uncle Hamish sighed. He untied the rope from the mooring rock and began to row. 'This is my niece, Euphemia Gillies.'

'How are you, Effie? Becoming bolder, I see,' said Frank Mathieson. He ruled St Kilda on behalf of Lord MacLeod, the island's landlord.

'If by bolder you mean faster.'

He laughed. 'Allow me to present the Earl of Dumfries and his son, Lord Sholto. They are great friends of Lord MacLeod.'

'It has been an ambition of mine to get over here,' the earl said brightly. 'I am a keen birder, you see.'

'Yes.' She could feel the younger man watching her keenly as she talked. As the others spoke, she had no such chance to look openly at him. 'Will you be staying for long, then?'

Mathieson inhaled. 'Well, a lot will depend upon the weath—'

'Certainly a week,' Lord Sholto interrupted. He allowed a smile to brighten his features as she finally met his eyes.

'A week?' Effie smiled back at the blue-eyed, golden-haired man. Finally she could see his face. And she liked it.

Chapter Two

The next day was the second Wednesday of May and it dawned clear and bright.

The men had decided to take advantage of the flat sea. They would make the journey to the nearby island Boreray to pluck the sheep.

Effie had remained to act as guide to the earl and his son. For this, they would pay her two welcome shillings.

An hour or so after they had set off walking, she and the two men stopped.

'You are lucky to call this home, Miss Gillies,' the earl said, once he had got his breath back. There was a sense of wonder in his voice.

'Yes, I am.' She looked down upon her kingdom with pride.

'Have you ever left here?'

'Why would I do that, sir?' She gave a shrug. 'I have all that I need.'

After a moment, the earl said, 'Can I be honest with you, Miss Gillies?'

'I hope you will, sir.'

'Before we left, Sir John told me that he had received a letter from the islanders. He said you had all written to the government – asking to move to the mainland. Did you sign the letter?'

'I had to. We agreed we would either all go or all stay.'

'And if the government grants your request?'

'But they never do. That is why I agreed to sign. If you are ready, sir?' she asked, as she started to stand up.

He nodded and they all rose, setting off again.

She watched Lord Sholto. Briefly their eyes met and she had a sense of being lifted, of the ground dropping away beneath her. It made her stomach swoop. She didn't understand the feeling. She was a St Kildan. She was a daring climber who swung from the ropes without a care. Now, for the first time in her life, she understood what others felt when they watched her as a spider on the wall: the fear of falling.

Chapter Three

Effie took the book over to the single small window, to see better by the moonlight. THE SONGBIRDS OF SCOTLAND was written in handsome gold-stamped lettering. The spine was stiff, as if it had never been opened. Another gift from Mathieson.

She had decided to leave it this time. However, curiosity had got the better of her, as it always did. Anything that came from the mainland was hard to resist. This book belonged to a life she would never know. One that couldn't be lived here, on a rock in the ocean. For the first time, she felt a flicker of regret about her home.

She watched a seal swimming near the shore in the moonlight. Its dark head rose and dipped below the surface. She saw it disappear below the waves. Then it rose again in a rhythm.

Wait . . .

It was no seal. A man was out there and he was swimming the width of the bay. She sat straighter. There was only one person this midnight swimmer could be, of course. No one here could navigate water like that.

She watched, transfixed. She had never seen someone swim before. Some of the men paddled like dogs when they fell off the boat. This helped till they could grab on again. But this was nothing like that. He moved like silk.

Afterwards, he stepped into his trousers. He walked up the beach onto the grass. Effie watched as he stood and stared at the cottage. Her cottage.

She fell back against the wall. She bit her lip as she tried to understand what she had just seen. Without thinking, she clutched the book tighter to her chest, already forgotten. It was no longer the most precious thing she had been given.

Chapter Four

'Is that Boreray over there?' Sholto asked the next day.

'Yes. It is where the men have gone to pluck the sheep.'

He frowned as he looked back at the small island. 'So then what is that?'

'What is wha—' But as she said it, she saw it and she knew. She knew immediately.

Four miles across the water, two huge slabs of turf had been carved from the grass and turned over. They were each the length of three men. From this distance they looked like dark cuts, a wound in the land.

It was a moment before she could reply. Only once in her lifetime had this signal been used.

'It is for sending the boat. One cut means they are ready to come back. Two means there has been an accident or someone is sick. Three means there has been a death.' She looked back at the island, already preparing to run. 'I can't stay, I am sorry. I have got to get back and tell the others.'

*

Donald McKinnon's limp body was carried between them. His injured head hung back. His skin was cloud-white. His pregnant wife sank down beside him.

'It is all right, Mary,' Lorna MacDonald said quickly. She was a trained nurse who lived on the island. 'He fell against a rock. He has got a nasty cut to his head. It is deep but it isn't bleeding out. As long as we can keep it clean, and he rests, he should be well.'

Sholto reached for his jacket in the boat. There was a rip in his shirt by the shoulder. As he turned, she saw great smears of blood across the front of it. His face was flushed and he looked utterly spent. She guessed he had never had to row an eight-mile medical emergency before.

He trudged up the beach to where she stood.

'Thank you,' she said quietly.

'Why are you thanking me?'

'For helping Donald and Uncle Hamish.'

He frowned. 'What kind of a man would I be if I hadn't?'

They walked together up the path, neither of them speaking. The silence between them seemed swollen with unsaid words.

Chapter Five

'Ready?' the earl's son asked, holding his hand out for Effie's. She had told him earlier that she couldn't swim – that none of them could. He had decided to teach her.

Without pausing Sholto led her barefoot over the stony shore. He tugged her along into the icy water. She gasped and shrieked, but her legs kept moving. As the water grew deeper it tangled around her knees, bringing her down. She landed with an almighty splash. She came to the surface moments later with wide eyes and a lungful of air. 'Oh! Oh!' she gasped, laughing. She was close to panic from the shock. 'That is *so* cold!'

She lay back. Her toes stuck out of the water. She felt his hands upon her shoulders, a support for her.

'There? It is not so bad, is it?' Sholto asked. He looked down at her as he began to walk backwards slowly, pulling her along. 'Keep your mouth closed – your eyes too if you like. Just get used to the feeling of floating in the water.'

Effie did as he said. However, she was too aware of his eyes upon her and she opened them again.

For a moment they fell still, eyes locked. Time seemed to stop as the formality between them began to crack. Within seconds, they were having a full-blown water fight. They slapped the sea with their palms and pushed waves at each other. The sound of their games echoed around the glen like the cry of an eagle.

Chapter Six

'Miss Gillies! I have been searching for you.' The voice was sharp through the air.

Effie and her friend Flora looked up. They saw Mathieson striding towards them.

'Eeesht,' Flora said under her breath. 'The devil himself. I will catch you later.'

Mathieson gave a short smile. There was something unnatural in his manner.

'His lordship has said how pleased they have been with your efforts. He wanted me to thank you for them.'

Effie's heart gave a flutter of panic. 'You make it sound like they don't need me to help them any more.'

She tried hard to think of a way to talk him round. She didn't want to lose her chance to see them – to see him.

'But what about my money?' she blurted. 'I was promised two shillings. I haven't earned it yet.'

That strange, awkward smile sat upon his face again. He paused, then reached into his pocket.

He fished out two coins for her. 'You are quite right. You deserve to be rewarded for all you have done. I will make sure his lordship knows upon my return.'

He stepped forward and tipped the coins into her palm. 'A word of advice. The power you hold is only an illusion. Don't play with a man's affections, Miss Gillies. Tread carefully.'

She watched him walk away down the slope. Her heart clattered in her chest.

Tiny, the bull, snorted heavily over the wall, making her jump. She would feed him later. However, it wasn't the bull she was frightened of.

Chapter Seven

It was later the same day. Flora's eyes seemed to catch on something over Effie's shoulder. She sat straighter. 'Who . . . ?'

Effie twisted to look. Sholto walked closer, and she rose to greet him. There were questions in his eyes, as there were in hers.

This is my friend, Miss Flora MacQueen. This is Lord Sholto . . .' She realized she didn't know his surname.

'Crichton-Stuart,' he said. 'Miss MacQueen, I don't think I've yet seen you in the village?'

'No, sir. I am spending the summer with Mhairi McKinnon with the livestock over in Glen Bay.'

'We haven't explored there yet,' Sholto said, looking at Effie. 'Perhaps that can be tomorrow's trip?'

Effie stared at him. 'I am afraid I can't, sir. Now the men are back, Mathieson will continue guiding you.' She looked away.

Sholto gave a small, embarrassed laugh. 'It is

our loss indeed. I know my father will be terribly disappointed.'

'I am sorry, sir,' she said awkwardly. She made no move to say anything more.

There was another pause.

'I ought to get back,' Sholto said. 'It has been a pleasure meeting you ladies.'

'Good evening, sir,' Flora nodded.

'Miss MacQueen.' He looked back at Effie. '. . . Miss Gillies.'

She didn't look up again till she saw his feet moving off.

Flora whirled on her heel when they were out of earshot. 'What is going on?' she demanded. 'I saw how you both looked at each other. This can only have one ending, and I don't want to see you get hurt. The stakes for him are different than they are for you.' She gazed at Effie with soft eyes. 'This rarely ends well for girls like us.'

Effie felt sadness sweep over her. 'Then what do I do?'

'Nothing. Let Mathieson do the guiding till the storm makes them leave. All you have to do is stay out of sight. Keep away from him till then. Can you do that, Eff?'

Effie blinked back at her oldest friend. Could she?

17

Chapter Eight

Colour was beginning to creep into the day. The sky grew brighter with every passing minute. It was utterly silent up here. The world slept at Effie's feet. Her collie Poppit – brown-faced with a white patch over one eye – sat beside her, ears up.

'Miss Gillies, you are a very fast walker,' Sholto panted. He placed his hands on his thighs as he tried to get his breath back.

She stared at him, amazed. 'What are you *doing* here?'

He sighed and smiled in the same motion, his head tipping to the side. 'I was swimming in the bay when I saw you sneak out from your house.'

She stared at him in disbelief. It wasn't even dawn! Did he never sleep?

His eyes burned into her. 'You looked like a wild rabbit just now. Why are you out walking at this time?'

'I am going over to Glen Bay.'

A flicker of a frown crossed his face. 'To be with your friend?'

She nodded. 'She needs help . . . with the sheep.'

He looked like he didn't believe her. 'It is an early start . . . Lucky I was swimming then or I might not have seen you.'

'Yes, sir.'

He winced. 'Please . . . none of the "sir" nonsense.'

She looked away. There was little point in arguing about it now.

There was a short silence.

'Our captain says we must leave on the tide tonight.' He ran a hand through his damp hair. 'Apparently a storm is coming.'

She pulled at a tuft of grass. It gave her something to do, somewhere to look. 'Yes, I know.'

'You know?' His eyes narrowed. 'And yet still you went? Without a goodbye?'

'I didn't think you would worry one way or another about my goodbyes, sir.'

A small laugh of disbelief escaped him, followed by a pause. '. . . But we are friends, are we not?'

'. . . If you say so, sir.' There was a tremor in her voice.

He looked pained now. 'Effie, don't call me "sir".'

'Why not? It is what you are.' She felt the anger

19

begin to overflow. She was eighteen years old. But she felt ragged and worn. 'You are a lord and I am just a wild thing. A wild rabbit.'

'No.'

'That is what you just said.'

'I know what I said,' he cried. 'But you must know there is a difference between what I say and what I mean? That there are things I can't say even though I . . . I would like to?' He moved towards her, but Poppit gave a low growl. He stopped and looked at the dog. Looked back at Effie. 'But if . . .'

'But if what?' She stared back at him boldly. She wanted him to say it, to make the words real. To give shape to the gap that stood between them. He had to go. He came from a bigger world than hers.

'But if I am to leave here tonight, then perhaps they should be said.' He watched her head snap up.

Effie felt her heart begin to pound. Poppit growled and Sholto looked at her again warily – but the dog wasn't looking at him.

'Friend! Not foe!' a voice called from below, making them both jump.

Sholto leaped to his feet. 'What?'

The sound of footsteps became distinct and then they heard laboured breathing . . .

Effie scrambled to her feet, trying to see further, better, sooner.

'Who is it?' she asked.

'Friend not foe,' the voice said again, closer now, with a weary sigh.

Sholto and Effie watched in silence. Their unwelcome intruder finally arrived over the blind summit with a smile. 'Well . . . Good morning!'

Chapter Nine

For several moments, no one spoke. They just watched Mathieson pant and sigh. His head was bowed, hands on his thighs, as he got his breath back. Effie wanted to cry. What . . . ? What was he doing here?

Their eyes met again and she saw the urgency in his. The clock was ticking. This time tomorrow he would be gone.

'I understood you had gone for a swim, sir. What made you follow Miss Gillies up here?' Mathieson asked him with curiosity.

There was a pause.

'Well, this is my last day on the isle. I hoped to persuade Miss Gillies to show me some of her roping skills before I leave . . . If you would be so kind as to serve as my anchor? Then Miss Gillies and I may descend together and she can instruct me better.'

The suggestion left Mathieson speechless. For once, he had been outwitted.

'Is that acceptable to you, Miss Gillies?' Sholto

asked her. 'Sharing an hour or two of your time before you leave?'

She tried to stop her eyes from shining too brightly. She would take whatever she could get. Flora could hardly be cross with her if they had Mathieson with them! 'Yes, sir. It is the least I can do. I feel I haven't earned my two shillings . . .'

Sholto's face changed as he remembered the matter of her payment. 'My word, I had quite forgotten. Here—' He reached into his pocket.

'Oh – no sir, it is already taken care of,' she said quickly. She didn't care for the money.

He looked up. 'Father's paid you?'

'Not the earl, sir. Mr Mathieson.'

Sholto looked back at Mathieson, whose face had flushed a deep red. '*You* paid Miss Gillies, Mathieson? When? . . . And why? This was a private arrangement between us and Miss Gillies.'

There was a pause. How could Mathieson avoid showing his desire to keep the guests to himself? 'It was after the drama with Donald yesterday. I didn't want you to be troubled after your great efforts. Miss Gillies was asking after it . . .'

Effie startled at how he twisted the truth. Sholto's eyes flitted upon her, seeing her silent protest.

Sholto simply smiled, his manner placid. 'I see. Well, that was very good of you, Mathieson. I will be sure Sir John hears of it.'

Mathieson's face changed. It was clear he had been expecting to be repaid.

'So, Miss Gillies, where shall we climb?' Sholto fixed her with a winning look.

They stood on the cliff face. A moment of silence whirled around them as even the birds were tuned out. Nothing else existed. Only the two of them.

She knew he was going to kiss her even before she saw the muscles in his forearm flex. He drew himself towards her. She closed her eyes as his lips met hers. The harsh, jagged landscape to which they clung became soft. Gravity ceased to have any meaning. She couldn't have said whether she was flying or falling.

When he finally pulled away, his eyes were aflame. 'All this, to get you alone.' He gave a low chuckle at their extreme situation. 'Although it seems fitting that I should kiss you where I fell for you.'

He had fallen for her? She felt her heart punching against her ribcage.

He kissed her again. 'I could do this all day,' he murmured when they finally broke apart. Both of them were breathless, wanting more.

Chapter Ten

'The whole village saw you,' Effie's father barked. 'Laughing and playing on the beach like you were children.'

She had gone for a swim with Sholto after the climb. She should have known that news of it would reach home before she did. 'And why shouldn't we? I have just spent the last three days with him and his father. We have talked all the while. We are friends.' She could feel her voice becoming strained, the tears pressing. Her feelings were too high to keep pushed down.

'*We* don't become friends with the likes of *them*. You mistook manners for something else. You have shamed yourself and me. Not to mention that Mathieson is livid. You have dragged his name through the mud too.'

'Why is it anything to do with him?'

'He is the laird's man! He will report back on you getting high and mighty, being too familiar with the laird's friends. You need to accept the natural order of things and understand where you belong. He is not one of our kind and you are not his. No matter how much you may like the look of one another. You can make eyes and play games, but that is not the ground for a real life.'

Tears were streaming down her face now. 'I just want to be free to live my life, instead of having labels put on me! I can't climb cliffs because I am a girl? I can't love him because I am poor?'

'That is not love!' her father shouted, his own voice becoming ragged with the strain. 'It is a foolish fancy, nothing more! And now you have brought shame upon me. You are a disgrace to our family. What would your mother think if she was to have seen this?'

Effie hid her face. Any mention of her mother felt like a slap.

'You will not leave here for the day. Stay where I can see you till that ship leaves and he is on it. You hear me?'

She pressed her face into her knees, crying silently and shivering. The chill after the swim settled in her bones.

'You hear?' he repeated, demanding an answer.

'. . . Yes, Father.'

Chapter Eleven

But later that day the supply boat came, and Effie was allowed out to help unload the cargo.

'My friends and neighbours,' Lorna MacDonald announced, 'you will be aware of the letter we sent asking for help with us leaving for the mainland.'

The group stirred as though they had been shoved.

'Well, today we have received our reply.' She held up a folded letter. '. . . And they have agreed! We are to be moved to the mainland!'

A shocked cry rang out.

Effie looked around to find Sholto staring at her. She was leaving here.

She was coming to live on the mainland, on his side of the water. The island life she knew here was going to be left behind. She would live in a different house in a different place and have a job. She blinked back at him, the two of them locked in a private world . . . If she lived differently, in a different place, would she be different too? Different enough to be good enough? For him?

'This is big news, Miss Gillies.' Effie turned to see Sholto standing beside her. 'How do you feel?'

Tears gathered in her eyes, the reality of it hitting her. She couldn't leave here! It was absurd. Unthinkable.

'Effie, I know it must be a shock. I know this is all you have ever known . . .' He cleared his throat, returning with a whisper. 'But could it not also be—'

'Miss Gillies.' Suddenly Mathieson was beside her. 'Please tell me you people had the decency to let his lordship know before you petitioned the British government?'

'Mathieson, there is no need for that tone,' Sholto said sharply. 'I understand feelings are running high. Everyone is rightly shocked, but Miss Gillies is not responsible for this. It appears that Miss MacDonald is overseeing the events. You may wish to discuss the details of it with her.'

It was a dismissal, they all knew.

Mathieson glowered like a hot coal for several moments. Effie wondered whether his temper would take him over again now. But he regained just enough self-control to walk off without another word. His manners were fast disappearing along with the future of his career.

Chapter Twelve

The note had said *'Meet me at the storm hut from this morning. I will be waiting for you'*.

Now she felt her blood pressure fall as she staggered backwards.

What . . . ?

'His lordship's not here,' Mathieson said, stepping out of the hut. He slapped her then, hard. 'You are a whore, Effie Gillies, and now everyone knows it. You have brought shame on your father. On your family name.' He gave another joyless laugh. 'And yet, still I am prepared to forgive you. To give you a chance of a good life. Am I a madman? Am I?'

He pointed to something lying on the ground by their feet. The broomstick was a dark shape she hadn't noticed before now. His grip tightened around her arm so that his fingertips touched.

'Yes! Now, Effie – jump!'

Her feet left the ground and she felt herself fly – for a moment. They landed again not a second later but in that wink of time, her entire life had changed. She was no longer Effie Gillies. She was Mathieson's wife.

Mathieson grinned back at her in the darkness. 'You are mine now.'

She was down and another scream tore through the sky – but it was several moments before she realized it hadn't come from her. Effie looked up from where she lay fallen on the grass. Poppit was attached to Mathieson's calf. Her teeth were sunk deep into his flesh. He howled in agony as she brought him down.

'Poppit!' Effie cried. She scrambled back, away, trying to stand on shaking legs. 'Poppit!'

Then Mathieson's bloodied leg lifted and wheeled around, connecting his boot to Poppit's body. Poppit slammed against a boulder with force, falling to the earth and lying limp.

'Poppit!'

'I will be back for what is mine! Lawfully *mine*, do you hear?' Mathieson spat, his face pressed against hers. 'We've jumped the broom and that makes you my wife now. I will take what is owed to me – if it is the last thing I do!'

For several moments she lay stunned.

She stretched an arm. 'Poppit?' she whispered.

The hazelnut coat didn't stir – but for a tiny twitch of an eyelid. A low whimper brought a sob from her.

'Oh, thank God!' Effie crawled on her hands and knees to where her pet lay. She dropped her face into Poppit's coat and wept. Poppit was alive! They both were . . . But what sort of life was this, now she had lost her freedom and her name? He was coming back for her. How could she smile or rest or know a moment's peace? This wasn't over. Far from it. The worst was yet to come.

Three months later: 29 August 1930

After

Chapter Thirteen

They were drowning the dogs.

The boat bobbed and the villagers streamed down to the jetty. Meanwhile, the dogs were having their heads held under a calm sea. Hounds that had herded their sheep and sat by their chairs every evening. Bubbles escaped in silent protest.

The process was quick, but it was no comfort to Effie.

'I will not let them kill Poppit!' She looked across and saw the white-uniformed navy men standing now beside her father. He was listening as he waved his stick angrily in her direction.

A couple of the men – Uncle Hamish and Angus McKinnon – were coming for her.

With a burst of power, she scaled the last stretch of cliff. She heaved herself onto the grassy slopes with a cry of effort. Poppit squealed and wriggled free in the next instant. The dog broke into an excited, clumsy run.

On her hands and knees, Effie scuttled back and

looked over the cliff. The men were advancing quickly.

'If you let me bring Poppit, then whatever we get for our cow at auction – once we have bought the licence – we'll give you both the rest to share.'

Both men stopped from sheer surprise rather than obedience. Their sunburnt faces were turned up to her.

Uncle Hamish paused for a moment. 'Yes, you have our word. Get down now. Enough of this nonsense. Heap no more shame upon your father.'

Effie's eyes flashed but she had her agreement. Her uncle had honour. Everyone knew his word was his bond. She scrambled to her feet. 'Come on then, girl,' she said, looking back.

Looking around.

'Poppit?'

A short bark, turning into a squeal, made her head whip round.

'*Poppit?*'

A silence came back at her as she stared into the distance from where the sound had come. There was a shallow dip over there, near the storm hut.

A dark head appeared. Broad forehead and heavy brows above hard eyes and a thick beard.

'Where is my dog? Where is my dog?' she screamed as Norman Ferguson, her friend Jayne's husband, strode towards her. 'Hamish has agreed! She is to come with us! It is agreed! Where is she?'

She saw his face – cold, unmoved – and knew it was already done. Shock and disbelief overtook her. How long had she been turned away from Poppit? One minute?

She screamed. Everything, all her efforts, had come undone in those few mere moments and she was alone now. Utterly alone.

'There is no money for her,' Norman said simply. He wasn't a bad man. Just not a sentimental one.

Chapter Fourteen

'Welcome to Scotland, Mr Gillies, Miss Gillies,' the man said with a brief smile.

Effie, weighed down by grief, didn't smile back. Part of her wanted to point out that they had always been in Scotland. They were every bit as Scottish as he was.

'My name is Mr Croucher. I will be escorting you to your new home today. Your carriage, Mr Gillies, Miss Gillies.'

Effie and her father stared at the vehicle. It was bigger than she had expected, and shinier too. What she liked most was that the wheels were so perfectly round. The only round things on St Kilda had been the stone mills used for grinding the barley. And they could only be described as round*ish*.

'Ahoy!'

The shout made them both stop and turn. Her Uncle Hamish was waving down from the deck.

'Where is Mathieson?' he called down to someone on the pier.

'Not here,' was the reply.

Hamish looked to the other men working alongside him, but they muttered back the same. 'Not here.'

'He has my money!'

'Not here.'

Hamish gave a reluctant nod, pulling back from the rails. His scowl made plain he was displeased.

'What was he doing entrusting money to that man anyway?' her father muttered, shuffling into the car.

Effie sat beside him without comment, her hands flat on the smooth seats that were the colour of plums, her heart beating fast.

Chapter Fifteen

'Be careful as you go,' Mr Croucher warned. 'The light's fading fast now and I am afraid there is no electricity here as yet.'

He lit a candle-holder set on the deep window-sill. Pale amber light lit up the front half of the room.

She looked around at the gloomy place. Perhaps it was a good thing that the damp was so bad and the light so poor. They couldn't settle here, and now her father would see it too.

The sooner they left, the better.

'Perhaps it is not *all* so bad?' Jayne Ferguson said. Effie glanced over to find her friend smiling at her. Jayne's hands were moving rapidly. Click-clack went the knitting needles, their bone heads dipping and bobbing. Old habits would die hard. 'Let's give this side a chance before we condemn it to eternal damnation. They may not have cliffs and seabirds here, but there is a different beauty in trees and songbirds.'

'Maybe . . .' Effie said. 'I have an early start tomorrow.'

'At the factory? Yes, I will see you there.'

'No, Jayne, the forestry,' Effie corrected her. 'You have got a man to feed you. In our house, *I am* the man and I need a man's wage. Da won't eat if I don't earn.'

Jayne gave another of her patient smiles. 'Ah, yes. Of course.'

'See you tomorrow, then.'

Chapter Sixteen

A flicker of amusement danced through the foreman's eyes. 'Well, Miss Gillies, I am sorry to have to inform you we only employ men at the forestry commission.'

'It isn't women's work I am after, sir. I need a man's wage. It is just me and my father, you see. He isn't good on his feet now, so it is up to me to put the meal on the table. You will see I am as hard-working and strong as any of these men. You will vouch for me, won't you, friends?'

A silence grew as no one stepped forward. No one spoke out. She felt her stomach lurch as their silence – betrayal – changed into something firm. Denial.

'Things are different here, lass,' the foreman said as her cheeks grew red. 'What may have been acceptable – necessary even – over on the islands, can't be done here.'

She could hear the low whirr of the spinning wheels, the clack of the looms, before she had even stepped through the door.

'You are Euphemia Gillies,' a stern older woman said.

'Yes.'

'I have just been hearing about you. Mr Lennox rang ahead, saying you had caused trouble at the forestry.'

'I didn't cause anything! I went seeking employ—'

The sudden slap stung her cheek. For a moment she thought she had been hit with a paddle.

'You have a tongue on you, I can see that. And there is fire in your eyes.' The woman was staring at her through narrowed slits of her own. 'You're trouble, Effie Gillies. I know your sort. Don't flatter yourself that you are special. You would do well to understand folks have put themselves out for you. Homes have been found. Jobs too.' She nodded at the weaving machinery set up behind her. 'But there will be no favours either. No talking back, no shirking, no arriving late. You will work hard, and to my rules. Otherwise there will be no work at all. Am I clear?'

Effie's eyes watered. If there was going to be a meal for her father's table tonight, she had to nod. But she could see in this woman's eyes that she wanted more than a 'yes'. She wanted submission. She wanted Effie's shame. A line had been drawn in the sand. Effie knew she would get no peace from this woman now.

Finally, she nodded.

Her friend Flora came over. She seemed to be limping. She clutched Effie's hand in her own while smoothing her reddened cheek with her palm.

'Sssh, you need to keep control of yourself,' her friend said. She steered Effie away towards a corner. 'It doesn't have to be for ever. Just let things be for a wee while. Let the waters settle. I know it is hard.'

'*Hard?* I have left my home and seen my dog killed. And all so that I could live in a house worse than the one we left? Up a track with only Norman Ferguson for help? Doing a job that will kill me within the month?'

Flora frowned. 'Why should it kill you? There was nothing as dangerous as climbing the cliffs.'

'The boredom, Flora! I will die of being indoors! Of wearing these damned boots all day!' Effie watched the shuttles pass across the looms, biting back furious tears. 'It is all right for you. You're engaged. You can swallow this knowing James has something better waiting for you. But –' she met her friend's gaze – 'I can't stay here. I have to leave. I have to find somewhere else.'

Chapter Seventeen

That evening, after washing and dressing, she opened the bedroom door and headed for the kitchen. As she stepped through the lobby, she caught a glimpse of something vast and shiny. She was in the other room before her brain had worked out that it was a car. And that the man talking to her father wasn't their neighbour, Norman Ferguson.

He greeted her with a look of relief. She remembered he spoke not a word of Gaelic and couldn't therefore communicate with her father.

'Your Lordship!' she exclaimed.

'Miss Gillies, there you are. I was just asking after you.' The Earl of Dumfries was wearing an expensive suit and a hat. 'What a pleasure it is to see you again. I hope you don't mind me arriving so suddenly. Miss Gillies, I call today because I would like to offer you a job. I want you to come to Dumfries House and curate my collection of birds' eggs.'

'What?'

Lord Dumfries smiled. 'You would be given lodgings on the estate in Ayrshire, several hours south from here. And a decent wage, of course.' He named a sum that made Effie's mouth fall open. It was more than the men were paid at the forestry.

She felt her blood rush. This proposal was more than she could have dreamed – getting a man's wage for doing what she loved. Being in the earl's employ gave her the very escape she had hoped for.

She shook her head slowly. 'I am sorry, sir, but I can't leave my father.'

'Of course you can't! And you must not! It was never my intention to separate you from him. Where you go, he goes. There would be room for you both, naturally. We will most surely have a cottage on the estate that could be made ready for you both.'

She blinked, marvelling at how easy everything was in his world.

The earl put his hat back on and looked at her. 'So that is a yes, then – yes?'

Her mouth parted. But what other choice did she have? They couldn't stay in this place, and she couldn't earn enough for the two of them on her woman's wage here.

'So long as my father agrees, sir. I will need to discuss it with him first. It is only right.'

*

46

She and her father watched as the earl passed through the garden gate and stepped into his gleaming car. The door was held open for him by a man in uniform with silver buttons.

'So? Are you going to tell me what that was all about?' her father demanded. He pulled his pipe from his jacket pocket and dangled it from his lower lip.

'He offered me a job,' she said quietly. 'Organizing his bird egg collection. He is prepared to pay me a man's wage. But we would have to move to a cottage on his estate in Dumfries. It would mean leaving here. I said I would have to ask you first. It is your decision, Father.' Her heart thudded as she gave away control of the choice. She didn't know what frightened her most – if he would say yes, or no.

He was quiet for several moments as he lit his pipe. 'A man's wage, you say? And we would have our own cottage?'

'That is what he said. But in Ayrshire, a hundred miles from here.'

Her father's eyes rolled over the damp stone walls, the rough floor, and the barren landscape outside the window. 'Tell him yes, then.'

She felt her heart gather into a gallop. 'You are sure?'

'If it comes down to being hungry here or

well-fed there, then I am sure. We need the money now.'

She swallowed. 'But what about Old Fin and your other friends?'

His lips turned down. 'What about them? If they are two hundred yards away and I can only walk twenty, then they may as well be two hundred miles away.' His voice was flat, his eyes hooded with despair.

Chapter Eighteen

'Your laundry and linens will be washed once a week, on a Thursday. Make sure they are in the basket by Wednesday night.'

'Oh, I can do my own.' Effie had never had anyone else wash her clothes before. The idea of it was strange.

'That would be unhelpful,' Mrs McKenzie said sternly.

'Oh.' Effie nodded. The housekeeper made 'unhelpful' sound awful indeed.

'Breakfast is at seven. Dinner at twelve. Tea at six, not a minute later or you will go without. Mrs McLennan runs a tight ship. The days are busy enough without being kept waiting for others.'

'Of course.' She turned to face the housekeeper. 'When will our cottage be ready, do you know? I must make plans for my father to travel.'

He had stayed behind for the short term. The cottage which had been chosen for them on the estate needed some work before they moved in.

'I can't say, Miss Gillies,' Mrs McKenzie said.

'That is the area of Mr McLaren, the estate manager. I concern myself only with the running of the great house. I will leave you to settle in. My office is downstairs, second on the left.'

Stairs. Even they were a novelty.

Shortly afterwards, she lay back on the bed. It creaked. She could hear distant voices. The sound of glass bottles rattled somewhere down the corridor. Footsteps crunched over gravel – a household in motion.

His household. *His* home. Could she really be in it? She couldn't sense him here at all.

Chapter Nineteen

In the servants' hall, eyes grazed up and down the length of her as they took in their newest member.

'I heard a funny thing,' one man said. Everyone was growing bolder as her novelty value broke through their shyness. 'That you are an island community, yet none can swim.'

She nodded, seeing the scorn in his eyes. 'Yes, that was largely true. Often the water's too heavy for fishing or swimming. But I can swim now. I had started to teach the children before we all left the island. If we had stayed, we would all have learned. I would have seen to it myself.'

'How did you *suddenly* learn to swim?' Mr Graves, the butler, asked.

She shrugged. 'Sholto taught me.'

Every set of eyes around the table widened.

'What?' she asked, seeing their shock.

No one replied. She caught the looks that flew between the staff. She saw that somehow she had confused them all.

'When will Sholto be back from London?' She couldn't delay asking any longer. She didn't care what they thought of her. Let them think she was wild, savage, odd . . . It was the only thing she wanted to know. She was here. How long must she wait?

'*Lord* Sholto is expected back tomorrow, Miss Gillies,' the butler said. 'Though he may be delayed. Apparently your old landlord's agent has gone missing. No one has seen Mathieson since before the island was cleared. Lord MacLeod is in a flap wanting to know what has happened to his man. It is quite a drama.'

Effie felt the blood drain from her face, a twist in her guts.

Frank Mathieson was still missing? It could not be.

She tried to gather her thoughts, scattered though they were like broken glass. 'The food is too rich for me,' she whispered, scarcely able to get the words out. 'Please excuse me.' And she stumbled from the room, leaving the servants gawping in her wake.

She burst outside. It was raining hard and she was glad of it. Her legs gave out as she saw what this meant. Her hands fell into the mud as she tried to catch her breath. She sat back on her haunches and tipped her face to the sky. She felt the raindrops on her face.

The tourist ship SS *Dunara* was to make a planned crossing three days after the islanders had left. It was the last of the season. The livestock had been shipped out and their small harvest already lifted from the ground. Natural resources on the island were even more scarce. The battle for survival was tipped in the wrong direction. It had now been eight days since the move – but she had calculated on a rescue within four.

She pressed her forehead to the wet ground and sobbed. Oh God. What had she done?

Chapter Twenty

In the library, her gaze was drawn to a beautiful yet strangely familiar book. She carefully lifted it from its stand, feeling the weight in her hands. It was a welcome distraction. She walked over to the nearest of the armchairs so that she could rest it in her lap.

A moment later, she screamed and the book fell to the ground, landing heavily face down.

'What . . . wha . . . ?' she gasped. She stumbled backwards into the side of another chair as a cheetah stared back at her. It had risen at her approach and was now sitting upright. Its lower jaw hung down as it panted. Around its neck was a sapphire-blue leather collar coated in jewels. A lead rested slack in the hand of a young, sleeping woman.

The woman was waking up. 'Heavens, you are awfully white. Should you sit down? You look like you may faint, dear. Would you like some tea? Or something stronger? I find a gin and tonic at this time very reviving.'

'I . . . I . . .' Effie's hands reached behind her. She grasped for the route around the chair. She couldn't take her eyes off the cheetah for a single moment.

'My name is Sibyl, Sibyl Wainwright, but all my friends call me Sid. You have got such a wicked tan. So where do you go?'

'Go?'

'In France?'

'Sid, what are you doing in here?' a voice echoed from the other side of the door. In the next moment it was opened.

Sholto walked in. His voice dropped as he saw Effie standing there, half hidden by a chair.

She couldn't blink. Nor breathe. Nor move.

'Effie.' The word was a croak.

'Hello, sir,' she mumbled.

'Sir?' Sibyl looked surprised. Her eyes narrowed, as if she had been duped. 'Why, the way you drifted through here, I thought you were a friend!'

It was a chance for Sholto to claim she was. However, the moment came and went before he even stirred. 'I . . . I wasn't . . . expecting you.' Just like that, his tan had paled.

'Your father didn't tell you I was coming?'

'I haven't seen him . . . yet . . .' He set off towards the drinks table. 'Would you care for a drink? I need a stiff—' He stopped abruptly again.

He was standing right in front of the empty book display. 'Sid?' There was an edge to his tone that made Sibyl sit up.

She followed his eyeline and gasped as she looked down at the book splayed on the floor. It had fallen in a spot half hidden under one of the chairs.

'I was just looking at the pictures.' Effie wasn't sure why the dropped book should create more fear than the beast sitting six feet away.

'Apparently that is rather a valuable one.' Sibyl shrugged. 'More "look, don't touch". It is one of only eight copies, made for the heads of the clans. One sold last year at auction for a record sum.'

Effie looked at Sholto, shocked. And Mathieson had given her one? And she had damaged another? Her heart was beating fast. She knew it was terribly wrong that one of these books should be in her possession. Sholto saw her upset and relented. 'Effie, it's fine. Don't worry, I will deal with it.'

'But your father—'

'It's only a book. I will tell him I dropped it.' He looked at Effie. 'Miss Gillies, it's fine,' he said stiffly. 'Accidents happen. My father won't care a jot.'

'I should go.'

She wanted him to implore her to stay but he

didn't stir. His expression was tight and closed. Without another word he turned away. He began to arrange the book as best he could on the display stand. Effie watched him for a moment. It was clear the prize book was a prize no longer, but what could she do?

Meeting Sibyl's amused gaze, she gave a polite nod and slipped from the room. Through the closed door, she could hear the woman's words at her back. 'Sholto, darling, where did you *find* her? She is a riot!'

Chapter Twenty-One

Mr Weir was writing at his desk when Effie knocked, having been summoned by him.

'Come in,' he said, not looking up. 'And close the door behind you.'

She did as she was told – and waited. She was nervous. Mr Weir was the big boss of the house – its steward.

'Sit down,' he murmured. He finished making his records in a log book, before finally looking up. 'Miss Gillies, I am tired from my journey. You will forgive me if I get straight to the point. I assume you have heard the news about Frank Mathieson?'

'That he is missing? Yes, sir.' She held herself very still.

'Do you know anything about his disappearance?'
She hesitated. '. . . No. Why would I?'

'I thought you were . . . close. Good friends.'

She felt her body grow cold. 'Mr Mathieson was our factor, Lord MacLeod's agent, and I respected him, sir, but I wouldn't say we were friends.'

'So he never brought you anything?'

Just from the way he asked it, she knew he knew.

'Well, once in a while he would bring books over – for our education. Our resources were so limited, you see. He was a kind man like that. But they weren't just for me. They were for all the children on the isle. Maybe that is what he was referring to?'

'Books.'

'Yes.'

'Nothing more?'

What did he know, exactly? Enough to suspect her involvement somehow. She sensed she had to keep as close to the truth as possible. 'Um, well, one time he brought some paint and brushes for us too. That was a wee while ago. But that was it. We relied on the kindness of friends, to better ourselves.' She sensed the last bit would satisfy him.

'He told me once he was courting someone special on St Kilda.'

The blood in her veins slowed to a crawl. *Courting?* 'Not me, sir. It must have been someone else. I was only a child all those years and that would have been wrong, would it not? It would be wrong even to suggest it.'

His eyes narrowed. 'Quite. Mr Mathieson may be a hard businessman but he is an honourable man.' He sighed. 'You should know Scotland Yard are now involved. Frank Mathieson is officially listed as a missing person. The police will be coming to interview you about what you know.'

'*Me*, sir?'

'Yes, Miss Gillies. I gave them your name as a person of interest.'

A person of . . . ? 'But why? I don't know anything!' she cried.

'Then you have nothing to hide.'

Chapter Twenty-Two

'Hello there, Mr Felton,' Billy, the hallboy, said. 'I thought we might find you here. This is Miss Gillies. She is going to be the new tenant of the cottage. Mr Felton is the gamekeeper,' he explained to Effie. 'He has agreed to restore the cottage for his lordship.'

'Well, I wasn't expecting to see you or I would have tidied the chippings,' Huw Felton said, glancing behind him. 'You must be wanting to see inside?'

'If it isn't too much bother.'

'No. Go in.'

He stepped aside. Billy took off. Effie led the way upstairs. She was amazed to see the cottage's creature comforts – a plumbed sink, radiators, an indoor bathroom.

She looked back out of the window. She wondered what winter looked like here. Was it all blankets of snow and crackling fires? Or howling gales, wind-whipped waves and ice on the beach?

'When will you move in?'

She shrugged. 'My father stayed behind to sell our livestock, but that is done now. If this is almost ready, then sometime in the next week.'

'It was a big thing, all of you moving over, as you did.'

So he knew she was a St Kildan? Word travelled, it seemed. 'Yes, it was. But for the best,' she said quickly. She knew he would ask, otherwise.

A sound came to her ear. 'What is that?' she asked. She twisted back to see a dark mass rocketing along the field.

Mr Felton didn't answer immediately. 'Someone out for a ride,' he said, straightening up.

It was too late for him to get downstairs, however. In the space of a few seconds, the rider had pulled the horse to a dramatic stop. It was now trotting in excited circles on the grass below. Its coat was a gleaming blackish brown, with chestnut nostrils and socks. It was also huge. Effie was not sure she would be able to see over its back, much less get up on it. She had never seen a horse close up before, nor in full gallop. There had been none on the island during her lifetime. Ma Peg had told her there had been a shire when she was a girl, to help with the ploughing.

Sholto stared up at them, breathing hard and flushed. He was wearing a tweed hacking jacket and a pair of brown riding trousers. His long black boots came up to his knees. He seemed to be unaware of the imposing figure he cut. He frowned at the sight of them both upstairs talking out of the bedroom windows.

'Miss Gillies. Felton,' he said briskly. 'Mrs McKenzie said I would find you here.'

'You want to see me, sir?' the gamekeeper asked.

'What? . . . No, no,' Sholto said, shaking his head irritably. 'Miss Gillies.' He scowled at the two of them. 'What are you doing up there?'

'I wanted to see the cottage before we move in,' she said quickly. 'My father will be down in the next week or so and I wanted to check it would be ready.'

The horse picked up its hooves and took two paces back. 'And does it fill the bill?' he asked, the reins slack in his hands.

'It is wonderf—'

'Felton, how much remains to do on it?'

'Another day of work, sir, that's all.'

'Right. Good. Well, that's something.' Sholto's manner was abrupt and distant. If she had thought their reunion in the library cold, this felt arctic. For the first time, Effie saw him as a lord, a landlord, an employer, her superior. A different man altogether to the bright-eyed, easy-smiling visitor of May. Why was he being so stony towards her?

The horse was still frisky from the gallop. Sholto walked it around, away from her. He walked it round in another circle to face front again. 'I am afraid my mother would like you to join us for dinner tonight.'

Effie was horrified. 'Me?'

'Yes, I am sorry. I know it will be dull for you, but she wants to hear all about St Kilda. My father's bored her rigid with it for the past few months. She would like to hear about it from a native's angle.'

Native? There was a short silence. She wondered if he realized how 'different' the word made her feel.

He patted the horse on its neck. 'He is thinking of buying the group of islands from Sir John, you see.'

'What?' The word escaped her as a bark, startling the gamekeeper. To hear St Kilda might be sold . . . ?

'Well, it's not much use to Sir John now, with no rent coming in, and Father's rather keen on the idea of turning it into some sort of protected bird sanctuary. I don't quite know all the ins and outs, but I expect he will tell us everything over dinner.' His horse took itself for another small

64

circular walk. He looked back at her over his other shoulder. 'So can I tell her you will come?'

Effie stared at him. Did she even have a choice? She nodded wanly.

'Good. Good,' he muttered. He was looking at her with an expression that could only be regarded as hostile. 'Mother will be most pleased.' But not him. That was the clear message.

He nodded, as if making to go, when he pulled back again.

'Uh . . . I should add – she has quite a nervous nature, the countess.' He paused. 'It might be best not to mention anything about her only son and heir dangling from a rope above the Atlantic . . .'

'Of course.'

'In fact, just don't mention the ropes, at all. It is irrelevant now anyway.'

She stared at him, knowing what he was really telling her. He was telling her that what had happened between them was irrelevant. Regretted.

'Of course,' she said again, her voice choked. 'I won't mention the ropes.'

His eyes narrowed, as though he was debating whether she could be trusted. 'Good. Eight o'clock, then. In the parlour.' He glanced back at the gamekeeper. 'Felton. Miss Gillies.' And with a jab of his heels, the horse took off again, hiding Sholto in a cloud of dust.

Chapter Twenty-Three

A maid called Fanny had helped Effie dress for dinner. In her fancy borrowed dress and new hair style, Effie hardly knew herself. Even just moving, dressed like this, was different. She used to only wear shoes every seventh day, and it was hard enough wearing them daily. But heels . . . she felt like she was balancing on pins.

Henry, one of the footmen, led her the short distance across the hall to the parlour. 'Good luck,' he murmured, one eyebrow arched and suggesting she would need it. He put a hand on the brass knob and turned it.

'Miss Euphemia Gillies,' he announced in a formal voice. He stepped back so that she might pass.

'Ah good, good!' She could hear Lord Dumfries's voice before she could see the man. 'Miss Gillies, I was just telling . . .'

His words fell like stones as she rounded the door and stepped into the room.

She reached the group in silence, wondering if

she had done something wrong already. 'Good evening,' she said in a quiet voice, her eyes naturally travelling towards Sholto. He was staring as if he had never seen her before.

'Good heavens, young lady, I never would have recognized you! I had to take a moment to check my eyes weren't playing tricks.' Lord Dumfries, recovering first, greeted her with a head bow. As if she were a lady. 'Last time I saw you, you had run through a hedge or . . . been for a swim, I think.'

'Your Lordship. My Lady.' She turned towards the older woman sitting at the far end of the sofa, who gestured for her to join her. Fanny had instructed her to greet Sholto's parents first. His mother was wearing a burgundy silk dress with silver threads. Her fair hair was worn upswept in the older style.

'Lady Sibyl.' Effie smiled at Sibyl. The young woman looked dazzling, both elegant and fashionable. Her glossy dark hair was styled in tight waves. She was wearing a sapphire satin gown with a cut like Effie's. At her neck were ropes of pearls, all worn at different lengths. Her lips were a vivid scarlet.

'Miss Gillies,' the countess said with a distinct note of surprise. 'My husband and son spoke of you after their trip earlier this summer. However, I am afraid they failed to mention you are a lady.'

Effie felt her cheeks sting pink at the compliment. 'Oh, no, I am no lady. I am from St Kilda. We are all equal there.'

There was an astonished silence. Effie could see Sholto hide a smile behind his drink.

Just then, the door opened. Effie felt herself freeze as Mr Weir came in. His eyes found her immediately, dressed above her station and sitting beside the countess. He walked straight over to the earl.

'I apologize for the intrusion but there is a telegram for you, sir,' he said quietly. 'It is urgent, I am afraid.'

'Read it for me, would you?' Lord Dumfries said to Sholto.

He handed the sheet of paper over. There was a momentary hush as Sholto cast an eye over it. '. . . Oh.'

'What is it?' the countess asked, sitting more upright at his tone.

Sholto looked up with a frown. 'It is from Sir John. It says his agent's body was found today on St Kilda. A tourist boat landed this morning and Mathieson was found on the beach on the far side a few hours later.'

The moon was full, bathing the room in a silvered light. Effie woke with a gasp. She closed her eyes but saw only the scene she had left the last time she had seen Mathieson. His body on the ground, blood on the rocks. Her eyes opened again, her gaze falling dully on the far wall. No, there would be no rest in sleep. She could do nothing but wait for the sun to come up.

Chapter Twenty-Four

Effie was heading for the garage late the following afternoon when she saw the gamekeeper coming from the woods. A pack of dogs bustled and ran around his legs.

'Miss Gillies!' he called. He raised his arm in the air to catch her attention.

She stopped where she was and waited as he altered course to come over. Only as he drew nearer did she see that the dogs were young ones. Barely more than puppies.

'Oh my goodness,' she whispered. She crouched, holding her arms out as they swarmed. They almost knocked her over. They had long silken black coats, with chestnut brown socks, chests and facial markings. She smiled – and it felt like cracking a nut. One dog in particular nuzzled into the crook of her elbow. Its muzzle was down, head pressed to her arm affectionately. 'And what's your name?' She stroked its velvety head.

'That one's Slipper,' Mr Felton said, coming to stand near.

She looked up at him. 'Slipper?'

'Aye. Because she's always under my feet.'

Effie smiled again. This time it didn't feel quite so strange. 'I like it. It suits her. How old are they?'

'Seven months now. They're getting leggy . . . and very rowdy.'

'What breed are they? I have never seen the like before.'

'Gordon setters. Intelligent, tame, soft mouths. Excellent gundogs. They have an instinct for the birds. His lordship would not have any other kind.'

He would have had Poppit, she thought, if he had known how clever she was. How attuned to the wildlife and birdlife around them. How loving and responsive and kind and brave . . . The sadness and pain surged in her again. How much had she lost? And for what exactly? She had gained nothing by being here . . .

Slipper was still nuzzling her, the other dogs losing interest as they picked up on other smells. 'Can I pick her up?'

'If you wish.'

She lifted the dog. She felt something inside her ease as she held the soft warm weight of the animal in her arms. The last time she had felt it, everything had been falling apart. She closed her

71

eyes, holding the puppy closer to her cheek. She popped her back down again.

'Where are you taking them?'

'On a walk. They need to stretch their legs. I have some pen mending to do so they can keep me company. You can too if you wish.'

'Thank you, but I am just on my way to the station to collect my father,' she replied. 'He is arriving here and I can't be late. He has no English.'

Effie entered the garage and found Sholto talking to the chauffeur. They were standing beside a glossy black car that had no roof.

'Oh, I'm sorry, I didn't mean to intrude.'

Sholto looked back at her as though she was testing him. 'Fraser tells me he is to take you to the station to collect your father,' he said irritably. 'I need to go to the station too, to collect a parcel. On the four o'clock. I ought to collect it personally,' he said quickly.

Was it the book, she wondered? Had it been repaired? Did he not trust her to take good care of it?

'There's room for three of us, though it will be a squeeze, but if we're taking your father back too, there won't be room for four.'

'Oh . . .' She felt she should bow out – but how could she let her father arrive in a foreign place, where he spoke none of the language, and she not be there?

She stayed quiet.

'I'm afraid there is only one thing for it, then. *I* will have to drive.' Sholto looked back at the driver. 'I am sorry, Fraser. I don't mean to deprive you of your duties.'

'Can't be helped, sir,' the chauffeur said. 'She is all ready for you.' He handed over the keys.

Sholto took them and looked back at Effie coldly. It made her stomach pitch and swoop, her blood still in her veins. '. . . Shall we, then?'

'You are very tight with Felton.'

He shot her a look, and this time there was more to see in his eyes. He wasn't cold at all, she realized. He was boiling hot, burning up. But with what? Rage?

The Auchinleck village sign flashed past the window. Already? The car moved so fast. She looked at him again. 'Sholto—'

'Don't get me wrong, it is good news. Very good. I can see it between you. He is certainly keen and you would be a good match together.' He nodded as if agreeing with himself. 'Shared interests, similar backgrounds.'

She couldn't believe what she was hearing. 'You sound like my father – marrying me off.'

He glanced over, seeing her rigid form. 'Oh, for God's sake, Effie, what do you want me to say?' he snapped. 'I never asked you to come here!' He indicated right and pulled up alongside the station front.

'No, your father did.'

'But he would not have done. Not if he knew.' He cut the engine and the car shuddered to a halt as he faced her at last, his eyes burning with an honesty that had not been there since she had arrived.

'Knew what?' She stared at him, her eyes growing wide as she understood his meaning. 'You mean if he knew that you kissed me?' Was it really so terrible? Was she that shameful?

'He wouldn't have you here if he knew what it risked,' he said in a low voice.

'What is it risking?' she asked, confused.

He looked away. The train was pulling into the station. People were walking through to the platforms. There was a loud hiss of steam as the brakes were applied.

He turned away, out of her reach and opened his car door. 'Forgive me. I shouldn't have said anything. It was selfish of me. You will be in the cottage now anyway. It will be fine.' He got out and shot her the briefest of glances. 'I will meet you back here when you are ready.'

Before she could say another word, he turned. He walked into the station, spine erect, shoulders back.

People were beginning to come through from the platform. Porters were carrying trunks and bags.

'Father!' With a start, she remembered why she was here. She jumped out of the car and ran through. Steam billowed as she looked up and then down the platform. She could see no sign of Sholto. It cleared just enough for her to catch sight of a man in the distance. He was making his way unsteadily, leaning heavily on his stick. Her father was stooped and seemed smaller than she remembered. Even his cloth cap seemed too big for his head.

She ran towards the frail figure with a gasp. Until that moment, she hadn't realized how much she had missed him. How much more she had left to lose. What would he do without her when justice caught up with her?

'Father!' she cried.

'Effie,' he breathed, looking relieved to see her.

She threw her arms around his neck and inhaled the smell of him – black twist tobacco and peat smoke. The smell of home. It was all too much. She began to sob for what she had lost, for what she had got back – and for what she could never have.

Chapter Twenty-Five

'Miss Gillies,' Mr Felton said, 'I have something I would love to share with you. I have no wish to alarm you. However, I know it will delight you. There is really no more time. It is now or never.'

'Delight me? Those are strong words, Mr Felton.'

'I am confident I can deliver on them.' He smiled and it lit up his eyes. It softened his face from the gentle frown it settled into at rest. 'It is just through here,' he said. He pointed towards the woods. 'Will you follow me?'

Effie felt herself tense. The last time she had found herself alone with a man she thought she could trust . . . 'It will be dark soon.'

'Which is why we must not delay.' He smiled, and she saw the man who sat and talked Gaelic with her father, who helped chop their logs.

'Fine,' she nodded.

A relieved smile lit up his face. 'Good. Follow me.'

They didn't stop walking till they arrived at a clearing.

'There,' he said, pointing. His eyes were trained on the rough cliffs opposite. A pine tree was growing out from the rocks at a strange angle. It was several moments before she noticed the large, twiggy nest.

She squinted, peering closer. Her breath held . . . It couldn't be.

For several seconds, neither she nor Felton stirred. Only when the parent bird began to fuss at the nest again did she dare to breathe.

'Osprey?' she whispered.

Felton just nodded.

'But they went extinct here fourteen years ago,' she whispered.

He nodded again. 'Until this summer.'

She watched as the young one sat on a branch, looking out to the distant sea. She could see the white spots on its back that distinguished it from its parent.

'The mother left a few weeks ago. They are getting ready to migrate. Any day now.' He glanced at her. 'It was why I had to bring you here, do you see?'

She nodded. 'Thank you. I am so grateful. I never thought I would get to see one. Have you shown the earl?' she asked quickly.

He shook his head. 'I don't approve of what he does,' he said quickly.

'You mean, collecting eggs?'

'Taking them just for display . . .'

She nodded. It chimed with what she had felt back home. An instinct she couldn't quite suppress as the earl had gathered egg after egg.

She looked back at the nest. 'So no one else knows?' she asked quietly. 'Just us?'

'Well . . .' He paused. 'Only Lord Sholto.'

Her head whipped round again.

He cleared his throat. 'Actually it was *he* who showed them to me. He brought me out here and asked me to keep an eye on them, to make sure they were protected from poachers. You can imagine the trouble we would have if word got out. The eggs would go for a fortune.'

'But he hasn't told his father? Even though they are on their own estate?'

The gamekeeper shrugged. 'He asked me to keep it between just the two of us. That was what he said. I shouldn't have broken my word to him by taking you here, but I knew you would understand how special they are.'

'I do. I really do.' She looked back at the birds that told her so much about the nature of the man – men – protecting them.

He placed a hand upon her own. She almost jumped at his touch. 'I am trusting you to keep the secret, Effie.'

Effie? It was the first time he had called her by

her given name. It was another step towards an intimacy she had known was coming. Nothing had been explicitly said yet. However, she saw it in his and her father's eyes when she came home to them in the evenings. An expectation was growing.

Chapter Twenty-Six

After a day's riding had almost ended in Effie falling from her horse, Sholto insisted that she have a stiff drink and a restoring bath in the big house before she returned to the cottage and her father. Mrs McKenzie, the housekeeper, filled a bath with hot water and swirling bubbles.

Effie stretched out her neck, dropping her ear to her shoulder on each side, before sinking back into the tub with a sigh. It really did feel so good.

A voice called through from the bedroom. A woman's voice.

Effie jolted in the water, twisting back to see Lady Sibyl walking across the carpet. She stopped at the door and looked without embarrassment, still wearing her riding clothes.

She came closer to the bath. 'Effie, I'm sorry. I want us to be friends, really I do.' Sibyl leant in closer. 'Can I tell you a secret?'

Effie blinked again. 'What?' she asked quietly.

'When we first met, I was jealous of you. The earl was forever telling me about this amazing young woman who had guided them on their trip. Then you turned up with that fantastic tan and figure.'

Effie could hardly believe what she was hearing.

'I know Sholto admires you terribly too, just like his father. He wants us to be friends. Can we? I was a silly girl for being so petty. And for galloping fast so that your horse followed and you were scared. Can you forgive me for being so beastly?'

'There is nothing to forgive, my lady.'

'Uh-uh. Sid.'

'. . . Sid.'

'Oh good!' Sibyl beamed suddenly, clapping her hands together. Her brown eyes shone. 'I am so pleased! And now to celebrate our new friendship you must come to the party tonight.'

'What? No!'

'Yes. You must. You absolutely must. Everyone is going to be there. I want to introduce you to them all. You will love them! They are such a riot!'

Effie felt steam-rollered. She had seen the young woman's excitement from afar. However, to be in the full glare of it . . . It was like sitting in a hurricane. But if this was what it was to be friends with her. If this meant she and Sholto could be allowed to be friends too . . . She knew he meant to avoid her again. Weeks might go by before she would even set eyes on him. 'All right.'

'Marvellous!' Sibyl beamed. 'I need to refresh and change my clothes, but come to my room when you are ready. Oh, this will be such fun!' She turned to leave and saw Effie's clothes lying in a heap on the floor. 'And I will give these to Jenny too, while I am at it.' Her nose wrinkled slightly. 'Then she can have them laundered for you, all clean for tomorrow.'

'That is really not necessary. I can do it.'

'Don't be silly. There are some stains here that will need some work if we are to get them out.' She inspected Effie's hand-knitted woollen vest before looking back at her with kind eyes. 'It is the very least I can do. Let me spoil you. I am trying to show you I am sorry, remember?'

Effie gave a wry smile. 'It is not that. I am grateful for all your kindness. But if you take those clothes – I have nothing to wear when I come out of here.'

'Oh!' She looked around the room quickly. 'Look, over there – there is a robe on the door you can put on. Come over to my room. We will find you some day-clothes too, although it may have to be a dress, I am afraid?' She pulled a face. 'I know you are not awfully keen.'

It was Effie's turn to smile. 'A dress is fine.'

'Super!'

Effie watched her go, a whirlwind of energy and good intentions. Suddenly she understood why Sholto always looked so tired in her company. It was hard work. She wondered what on earth she had just agreed to.

Effie stopped, stunned by the sight of herself in motion. She had never had any idea of how she looked before these past few weeks. It was one thing to sit in front of a mirror and look at a static image, like a painting. However, to see herself moving, in these clothes, through this house . . .

Now she could scarcely believe she was *her*. No matter that her heart was clattering beneath her ribs. That was not what the mirror showed.

The young dark-haired woman staring back was beautiful and poised. Effie suddenly realized who it was she had become. Even if it was only for tonight, she was the girl with the hand-drawn book. One who wore silk dresses and lived in this lovely house. There was no sign of her former self, dressed in patched clothes. She put a hand to her hair, to her lips, and slowly smiled. Perhaps she really could walk in there and belong . . . ?

Ahead, she saw Henry emerge through the doorway with a tray. He looked more flustered than she had seen before. He did a double take as he saw her. He looked shocked – the dark-haired wig, no doubt. However, his feet didn't stop. In the next moment, he went down the spiral staircase. It would take him to the servants' passage.

Effie took a deep breath. She moved forward into the heat and noise of the party.

She felt hands on her bare arms and shoulders as she passed. It was as though these people knew her. There was a man in front of her. He was wearing a red costume, with a blue sash.

'Excuse me,' she said, trying to get past.

The man turned and she found herself face to face with the king.

'Your Royal Highness,' she breathed.

The king stared back at her sternly for several moments. Had she said the wrong thing? Should she do something?

But then he laughed. He threw his head back and laughed. She saw the elastic holding on his beard around his ears. She saw his eyes were brown, not blue.

'And who have you come as, my dear?' he asked. He clutched a hand onto her elbow, stepping back to have a good look. 'Wait. Let me guess.'

Who had she . . . ? She looked around the room, seeing suddenly not clothes but costumes.

'Oh my goodness, I have got it!' he cried, eyes bright.

'*Effie?*'

She felt another hand on her arm and turned. She saw Sholto staring at her with a look of disbelief. And something else, too . . . concern?

'What are you doing here?'

She no longer had any idea what she was doing here. She had never imagined a party might be like this. She wanted to tell him she had come to show him she and Sibyl were friends. That she had come for him, but—

'My God, your hair . . .' he said quietly. He didn't think as his hand lifted to touch it. 'What did you do?'

A part of her brain wanted to ask if he liked it. And the dress too? That Sibyl had done it all for her so that they could be friends at last. Before she could, he spoke again.

'Did Sibyl do this?'

She managed to nod. Why wasn't he pleased?

'Effie . . .' His eyes lifted off her. He looked around the room for someone. Who?

'I say, Sholly old chap, who are you supposed to be?' the king asked him now. 'Is that not your usual get-up?' He gestured at Sholto's outfit of a black tailcoat and white tie.

'Lord Chatterley,' Sholto muttered.

The king laughed. 'Ha, splendid, old boy. Makes all the difference tonight. You would not catch me at knee-height to this crowd, I can tell you. I know you don't like these themes.'

'No, Ernest, I don't ,' Sholto said tersely. His eyes were already back on Effie. He looked desperate.

The king tapped his head. He got the hint at long last and wandered off into the crowd.

'Effie, you shouldn't be here,' Sholto said with urgency.

She felt her heart drop. 'But why not? Sibyl specially asked—'

'She shouldn't have,' he said firmly. 'It wasn't . . . it wasn't kind.'

'I don't understand. She has been nothing *but* kind. These are her shoes, her dress, her jewels, her hair . . .'

He was staring at her with a look she couldn't read.

The crowd pushed them together suddenly. His hands gripped her bare arms as people jostled to get past. Effie looked up at him. She was shaken and dazed by what was happening. She felt like she had been thrown into a writhing pit. Was this so very different to the minister's descriptions of hell? The crowd had a manic edge. It was as if everyone was teetering on the brink of hysteria.

She was aware of a growing hubbub, a steadily increasing din.

Sibyl's laugh carried over to them. To Effie's surprise it wasn't coming from the direction of the fireplace where she had said she would be. She wasn't already the focus of her two hundred closest friends . . . she was only just coming in.

Effie turned to see what was going on. She couldn't see past the wired, flowing scarf of Amelia Earhart. Instead, she saw a ripple in the crowd, like a snake swimming in a river. It made its way through, coming closer . . .

Laughs and shouts followed Sibyl's progress. 'But who *are* you?' someone called, as a sense of scandal took hold.

Suddenly, the snake was upon them. Effie gasped as Sibyl blinked back at her, almost unrecognizable. Her face was smeared with mud. Her hair was a wild tangle. Her clothes – a boy's shirt, vest and trousers – were covered with stains. Her feet were bare and a rope was looped around her torso. A dead pheasant dangled from it at her shoulders.

'What do you think?' she asked, flicking at the dead bird. 'I know it is supposed to be a seagull or whatnot, but I couldn't get one at such short notice. The gamekeeper was most helpful, though.'

'You are in my clothes,' Effie whispered in disbelief, looking her up and down.

'And you are in mine! It is just too fabulous.'

Effie felt her eyes sting with tears. She realized what Sholto had been trying to tell her. She felt the insult bloom. People looked between the two of them, slowly beginning to understand the ruse. She felt suddenly not beautiful but ridiculous to be made up as that woman. She was humiliated that Sibyl had shown her as some sort of savage. 'Why would you do this?'

'Darling, it is an impersonation party! I am you and you are me.'

'But you never told me that!' The words escaped her as a cry, revealing her hurt. Sholto looked over at her with a pained expression.

'Why, I thought it would be a surprise. Don't you love it?' For the first time Effie noticed a flatness to Sibyl's voice, a deadness behind her eyes. There had never been kindness or friendship in her actions. She was cruel.

'Sibyl, what the hell are you doing?' Sholto's voice was a growl, white spots of rage in his cheeks. 'You know this is completely unacceptable.'

Sibyl's smile vanished like the sun behind a cloud as she saw his anger. 'Why? Why is it? She is dressed as me. Why can't I be her?' Her eyes flashed. 'Is that not what you really want, Sholto? Her, but me? Or is it me, but her?'

He gulped at her bold words. The party beat

around them like it was a heart and they were a blockage. Something stuck. Something dangerous.

'Stop it,' he snapped. 'Not here, Sid. Not now.'

He went to turn away, but Sibyl lunged for him. 'No? Not the right time?' She had her hand on Sholto's arm. 'Tell me, then, seeing as timing is *such* an issue for you, darling. When exactly would be a good time to tell all our friends here that we are engaged to be married. That we have been for six months? Why exactly are we keeping it a secret? What are we waiting for?'

Her voice had risen to a shriek. Several people around them gasped.

One man pressed his hand to his mouth in pretend shock. His moustache twirled to point upwards, a monocle at one eye.

Effie flinched. He was gross. They all were. Even Sholto. Even in all his elegance and good manners . . .

Tears sat in her throat and pooled at her eyes as she looked across at him. It wasn't hearing he was engaged now that crushed her. It was that he had been engaged when he had come to St Kilda. When he had kissed her and asked her to make a plan . . . When he had found her on her rock in the sea, he was already lost to her.

And what had she suffered because of him,

aside from her own heartbreak? The jealousy he had spurred in Frank Mathieson had sparked a ripple effect. Mathieson was dead. Poppit was dead. Effie was left broken by what she had had to do to survive. Her entire life was in tatters for someone unworthy. She had invested in a lie.

She tore the wig from her head and threw it at him. His mouth parted as she stood before him, herself again, wild and defiant.

'You disgust me!' she cried. 'You aren't better than me! You are worse!'

'Effie—'

'Where is your honour?' she demanded.

Sholto cringed at the question. She wasn't interested in hearing his answer. She looked around for an escape route to the door. She couldn't breathe in here. She couldn't think.

'Effie, just wait—' Sholto reached for her, holding her back.

'Get your hands off me!'

'Don't go,' he begged.

'Better a good retreat than a bad stand,' she spat.

'Please! Just listen to me—'

'Sholto!' Sibyl's voice was broken with shock at his actions. 'What are you *doing*?'

Effie jerked her chin towards Sibyl. 'She is right. What are you *doing*?' she scoffed, her eyes blazing. 'People are *looking*!'

He looked back at her desperately. 'Effie – I can explain.'

'You both deserve each other.'

'No—'

'Yes!' she cried suddenly. 'Yes! Stop pretending there is a different ending! It was always going to be this way. You belong with her. And I belong to another anyway.'

His mouth flattened. 'Felton is not—'

'Not him,' she spat, cutting him off. 'You are engaged . . . and I am already wed!'

His hand dropped from her arm like he had been burnt, her wig falling to his feet. *'What?'*

The pain flared in his eyes and she was pleased to see it. He had treated her like a fool but she was nobody's victim. She felt her own tears threaten. They would not fall, not for as long as she stood here. Let him suffer for once! Let him know how it felt to lose!

She glanced at Sibyl. Without a word she turned upon her heel. She drove the satin stiletto into the cruel woman's bare foot. A scream pitched through the cedar-panelled room but Effie walked on. She was the only truly wild one in a room full of pretenders.

Chapter Twenty-Seven

The skies were clear, stars already peeping as Effie tore through the night, entering the garden maze. Sholto was somewhere behind her.

Bewildered, she ran on, taking a left turn, then a right. A left, a left, then another right. She climbed a fifteen-foot gate. Only to come to a towering stone column and a dead end. She stared at it in panic. Where was she? How did she get out of here? Should she turn back or find another way around?

There was a rattling of the gate. She knew he – a skilled climber too – was scaling it. There came the sound of him jumping down. After that, a moment of silence. She listened to the sound of her own breathing.

'Effie, I know you are in here.' Sholto's voice was raised, but also muffled. 'I am sorry you had to hear about the engagement like that. I wanted to tell you about it before I left St Kilda. I left a note at the bull house that night, as I said I would, asking you to meet me.'

She frowned. There *had* been a note from him? 'I waited at An Lag but you did not come.'

An Lag? *Not* the storm hut? Mathieson had switched the notes?

'I assumed your no-show was your answer. That you were facing up to a truth I didn't want to see. That you were better able to see the reality of our situation and act . . . in the right way.'

There was another silence. 'If I had known you were –' he cleared his throat – 'with someone else . . . Why did you not just tell me? It could have saved so much pain.'

Her head whipped up at the new direction of his voice and she saw him standing a few feet away, at the end of the path.

'Because it is not what you think,' she said quickly, her voice thick. 'It is not.'

He blinked, looking doubtful. He was holding his body stiffly, as though he was injured. 'Who is he? I have to know. Tell me his name.'

She felt herself begin to tremble. Even just talking about it made her want to fall apart. To disappear. 'It doesn't matter now. He's dead.'

She watched his expression change. '*What?*'

'He died.'

'When? How?'

She shook her head wildly.

'Effie, tell me his name.' He placed his hands

93

on her arms but she wouldn't look at him. His voice was hoarse. 'Tell me it was not . . . *him*.'

She looked up then. Her eyes were round and shining with tears. 'He took your note from the bull's house and replaced it with his own.' She faltered. 'It sent me to the storm hut, on the other side of the glen from you.'

Sholto's face crumpled as Mathieson's trick was revealed. 'No.'

'He was waiting for me there. He made me . . .' She swallowed. 'He made me jump the broom with him.'

'What?'

'He said it made me . . . lawfully his.'

The breath caught in his throat.

'But that is a lie! Broomstick weddings aren't legal!'

'Not here, perhaps. But your ways are not the old ways. It was different, over there. The law is . . . loose.'

He paled, watching her closely. 'Effie? What did you do?'

She was already far beyond his help. She took a breath. 'The night before we left the island, he caught me outside the kirk. He told me he was going to tell my father we were wed. He said he had been "reasonable". That he had given me that last week on the isle with my father. However, I would be going to the mainland with him. As his wife.'

Sholto blinked. 'What did you say?'

'I agreed with him. I had been braced for it for months. Ever since he went away with you that night, I knew he would be back. So I got myself ready. I planned for it. I tried never to be alone but I knew it was an impossible task. He would catch up with me eventually, one way or the other. Poppit wouldn't let him anywhere near me during the days. But all it took was a few moments alone outside the kirk that last night . . .

'So I told him I was happy with the marriage. I said I believed it was a better match than I could have hoped for. That he had been patient long enough.' She swallowed, trembling as she remembered her bold lies. 'I got him to meet me on the other side at midnight,' she said quietly.

'Glen Bay?' Sholto frowned. 'He didn't query being so far from the village?'

'I told him we should be somewhere private where we could . . . take our time and not be disturbed . . .'

Sholto winced, understanding perfectly.

'I got him drunk till he passed out, then tied him up. I put a knife out of reach, but where he could see it. I left him a sheep's bladder full of water – enough for four days if he was careful

95

– and some oatcakes. The SS *Dunara* was due a few days after we left, but . . .' She bit her lip. 'The winds got up and they were late in getting across. Too late for him.'

He frowned. 'So you didn't go there to kill him?'

'I just wanted to get away. But it led to the same thing.' She shrugged hopelessly.

'Yes, but motive matters, Effie! At worst, it is manslaughter, not murder. And you were afraid of what he was going to do. If this ever came to light, we could argue self-defence. That is hugely significant.' He was looking at her intently now. 'Think carefully now – were you seen?'

'I don't think so. It was dark and everyone was so busy.'

'Does anyone know what you did?' He looked back at her, desperation in his eyes.

She bit her lip. 'There is one person who might be able to . . . guess.'

'Who?'

'I asked one of the trawler captains to buy me some whisky from the mainland. There was never any on the island.'

'Hmm. I see no reason for the captain to link your whisky bottle with Mathieson's death. What did you tell him you wanted it for?'

'Doping the bull. For the move.'

A hint of a smile came into his eyes, gone again

in the next second. He looked away, his gaze distant, lost in his own thoughts. 'It has been a couple of weeks now since he was found and no one has come knocking. That must be cause for hope,' he said quietly. 'I will ask Sir John what the police know anyway. Find out where the inquiry is at.'

'Please, you must not interfere. The less you are involved—'

'If you think I am letting anything else happen to you on account of *him*—' His voice was sharp, but she knew it was not her he was angry with. Immediately, he reached for her hand and pressed it to his cheek. He turned his head and kissed the inside of her wrist. 'I am sorry. I am sorry. But I won't let him take you from me again, Effie. He did it in life but I will be damned if he does it again in death.'

She stared up at him. She saw his desperation to protect her and knew it was hopeless. The captain might not yet have any cause to connect her whisky with Mathieson's death. However, she felt Mr Weir would make the link soon enough. But there was no point in worrying Sholto with something he couldn't control. 'I will be fine. I am certain no one saw us. Like you said, they haven't come for me yet and every day that passes . . .'

He nodded urgently. He kissed her wrist again.

He held her like she was something holy, sacred and rare. Something to be protected, but not possessed.

He looked back at her with eyes full of sorrow and regret. How much had they suffered – lost – for these few sweet moments? How many more would they get to have?

Or was this it?

He looked back at her. Time stood still. She leant forward and kissed him. She felt the tension in his body as her story settled in him like rocks. She felt his wet cheeks against hers. She tasted the sweetness of his lips as he drew her closer. He kissed her the way he had on the rope, when they had been hidden from the world. When nothing and no one else existed. They were still hiding.

However, instead of clinging rigidly to rocks, she was not afraid to fall now. She let him pull her to the ground, sighing as his hands travelled over her. The lush grass was sweet in the night air. And the owl in a far-off tree called darkly for its mate.

Chapter Twenty-Eight

'She is gone,' Billy said firmly, the look in his eyes making it plain who 'she' was.

'Gone?' Sholto had done it, then? He had said he would – but so soon? Effie felt her soul leap.

'Yes. Fraser drove her to the station this morning.'

'Not Sholto?'

'No. Not him.' For once, he didn't correct her cheeky use of his name.

She stared down at the bundle, trying not to betray how fast her heart was beating. She knew her cheeks must look flushed, at the very least. Her happiness felt almost uncontainable. Was it contained – or could Billy see it in her? Was her secret nothing of the sort?

'Effie,' Sholto said as he approached her, pulling on the reins. She could see the joy inside him trying to escape, just as it did her. There was a basket balanced between his legs. He jumped down with it and threw the reins over the gate post. She stepped back to let him pass. His gaze fell to the bundle in her own arms. From his expression, he seemed to know what it contained too.

'A picnic?' she asked.

He hesitated. 'Not exactly. Look inside and see.'

With a nervous laugh, she lifted the lid. A cold wet nose popped out.

'Slipper?' she gasped. She reached in and pulled her into her arms. The dog wriggled happily. 'But what are you doing with—'

Another cold, wet nose appeared. She blinked. 'You have brought *two*?'

He beamed. It was that same smile she knew from St Kilda. Heady happiness.

She laughed. 'Sholto, what is going on? Does Huw know you have got them?'

'It was Huw who gave them to me. Or rather, I bought one and he gave me the other to give to you. As a gift.'

'But why is he giving me a gift?' she puzzled. 'I don't understand.'

'I went over there this morning. We have known each other since we were boys. I wanted to make things right with him. I had to.'

She swallowed. 'You mean . . . ?'

He nodded. 'I told him. About us.'

'Sholto.' Her voice had dropped to a whisper. 'You can't.'

'But I did,' he said firmly. 'And now I am going to tell everyone. My parents too.'

She shook her head, confused.

'Effie, I want you to be my wife.'

'Wife?'

He blinked. 'I mean it, Effie. I will not lose you again.'

'Sholto—' she protested. She knew she had to tell him about Mr Weir now, before he went any further. How he would surely soon suspect her involvement in Mathieson's death. Self-defence or not, there was no denying what she had done.

Sholto pressed a finger to her lips. 'I won't pretend it won't come as a shock to my parents. But they think you are delightful, and they want me to be happy.' His smile grew, eyes sparkling. 'Where is your father?' His eyes fixed upon the house.

Effie turned to see her father standing by the doorway. He was holding the other puppy – which had run through – with a puzzled look.

'She is for you, Father,' Effie said in Gaelic, walking over. 'Huw is going to train her up for you.'

'For me?' he asked. 'Why?'

She swallowed. 'For company.'

Her father stared at her, as if he had heard something more in those two words.

Sholto stepped forward. 'Mr Gillies, I love your daughter,' he said. In Gaelic!

Effie's mouth dropped open. Her father looked shocked, too.

'Would you do me the honour of allowing me to ask for her hand in marriage?'

A stunned silence met the question.

'Where . . . where did you learn to say that?' she whispered.

'Felton,' he murmured, never taking his eyes off her father.

Effie looked at her father too. Well?

He held her gaze for several moments. The silence between them was more profound than words could ever be. He had lost so much in his life and had precious few gains.

'Did I not always tell you – go courting afar but marry next door?' he said finally. He swept his arm from the cottage garden towards the great house across the fields.

She laughed. Yes, they *were* next door. Albeit with three hundred sheep and eighty hectares between them. 'You are sure, Father?'

He shrugged. 'He loves you, and he has sheep.'

'An earldom too. But yes, sheep.' With another laugh, Effie stepped into his embrace, smelling the peat fires of home still upon him. The two men shook hands solemnly.

'I wonder . . .' Sholto murmured, wandering over to the cottage.

'What is he doing? You aren't leaving me already, are you?' her father asked. He watched as Sholto disappeared inside.

'No, but . . .' She had no idea what he was doing. Then Sholto emerged a moment later with the broomstick in his hand. With a smile, he laid it down upon the ground by her father's feet. He looked up at him.

Her father nodded his approval.

'You know that is not lawful.' She laughed as Sholto took her by the hand and led her around.

'It is if we both want it to be. I will marry you any and every way I can, Effie Gillies.' His eyes shone and she knew what he was doing. This wasn't just honouring their island traditions – a nod of respect to the old ways. It was righting a terrible wrong.

'Will you jump the broom with me?' he asked.

She beamed. 'As many times as you like.'

About Quick Reads

"Reading is such an important building block for success"
~ Jojo Moyes

Quick Reads are short books written
by best-selling authors.

Did you enjoy this Quick Read?

Tell us what you thought by filling in
our short survey. Scan the **QR code**
to go directly to the survey or
visit **bit.ly/QR2024**

Thanks to Penguin Random House and Hachette and to all
our publishing partners for their ongoing support.

A special thankyou to Jojo Moyes for her generous donation in
2020-2022 which helped to build the future of Quick Reads.

Quick Reads is delivered by The Reading Agency, a UK charity
with a mission to get people fired up about reading, because
everything changes when you read.

www.readingagency.org.uk   @readingagency   #QuickReads

The Reading Agency Ltd. Registered number: 3904882 (England & Wales)
Registered charity number: 1085443 (England & Wales)
Registered Office: 24 Bedford Row, London, WC1R 4EH
The Reading Agency is supported using public funding by
Arts Council England.

Find your next Quick Read...

For 2024 we have selected 6 popular Quick Reads for you to enjoy!

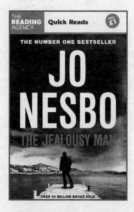

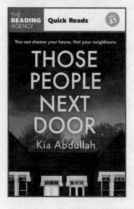

Quick Reads are available to buy in paperback or ebook and to borrow from your local library. For a complete list of titles and more information on the authors and their books visit **www.readingagency.org.uk/quickreads**

Continue your reading journey with The Reading Agency:

Reading Ahead

Challenge yourself to complete six reads by taking part in **Reading Ahead** at your local library, college or workplace: **readingahead.org.uk**

Reading
Groups
for Everyone

Join **Reading Groups for Everyone** to find a reading group and discover new books: **readinggroups.org.uk**

World Book Night

Celebrate reading on **World Book Night** every year on 23 April: **worldbooknight.org**

Summer Reading Challenge

Read with your family as part of the **Summer Reading Challenge: summerreadingchallenge.org.uk**

For more information on our work and the power of reading please visit our website: **readingagency.org.uk**

More from Quick Reads

If you enjoyed the 2024 Quick Reads
please explore our 6 titles from 2023.

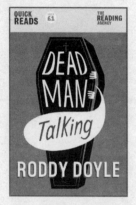

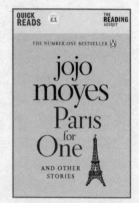

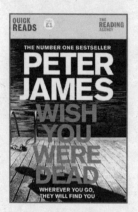

For a complete list of titles and more information
on the authors and their books visit:
www.readingagency.org.uk/quickreads

Look out for the next spellbinding story from St Kilda

The Stolen Hours

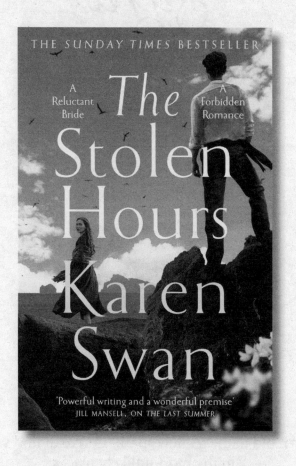

A reluctant bride. A forbidden romance.
An island full of secrets . . .

'A glamorous adventure'
Hello!

An old flame. A new spark. Love can find you
in the most unlikely places.

The Hidden Beach

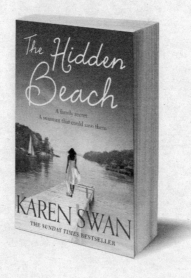

'Novels to sweep you away'
Woman & Home

Secrets, betrayal and shocking revelations await
in Sweden's stunning holiday islands . . .

The Spanish Promise

'The perfect summer read'
Hello!

The Spanish Promise is a sizzling summer novel about
family secrets and forbidden love, set in the
vibrant streets of Madrid.

The Greek Escape

KAREN SWAN

THE SUNDAY TIMES BESTSELLER

**'A beautiful setting and steamy scenes –
what more do you need?'**
Fabulous

Set on a beautiful island, *The Greek Escape* is the perfect
getaway, bursting with jaw-dropping twists
and irrepressible romance.

The Rome Affair

'Enthralling and magical'
Woman

The cobbled streets and heat of Italy's capital
come to life in *The Rome Affair*

Summer at
TIFFANY'S

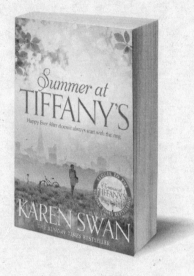

'Romantic'
My Weekly

A wedding to plan. A wedding to stop.
What could go wrong?

This Quick Reads edition published 2024 by Pan Books
an imprint of Pan Macmillan
The Smithson, 6 Briset Street, London EC1M 5NR
EU representative: Macmillan Publishers Ireland Ltd, 1st Floor,
The Liffey Trust Centre, 117–126 Sheriff Street Upper,
Dublin 1, D01 YC43
Associated companies throughout the world
www.panmacmillan.com

ISBN 978-1-0350-2914-3

1 3 5 7 9 8 6 4 2

A CIP catalogue record for this book is available from the British Library.

Typeset by Palimpsest Book Production Ltd, Falkirk, Stirlingshire
Printed and bound by CPI Group (UK) Ltd, Croydon, CR0 4YY

Visit **www.panmacmillan.com** to read more about all our books
and to buy them. You will also find features, author interviews and
news of any author events, and you can sign up for e-newsletters
so that you're always first to hear about our new releases.